For my children,

grandchildren,

and great-grandchildren.

www.mascotbooks.com

Smile and Say Hi

For more information, please contact:
Mascot Books
620 Herndon Parkway, Suite 320
Herndon, VA 20170
info@mascotbooks.com

Library of Congress Control Number: 2020921403

CPSIA Code: PRT0121A
ISBN-13: 978-1-64543-777-2

Printed in the United States

Smile and Say Hi

Mary Jo Hazard

Illustrated by
Srimalie Bassani

Michael Joe Bob was a prince of a guy.
He was smart, very brave, but remarkably shy.

Michael slew dragons and waged mighty wars,
But when someone came over, he stared at the floor.

"Smile and say 'hi' Mike," his mother would say.
"I can't," he'd yell, quickly running away.

He'd run straight to his room and slam the door tight,
Jump into his bed, and pretend it was night.

One day his dad said, "I know that you're shy,
But tomorrow in school, Mike, please give this a try.

Just smile and say 'hi.' There's no reason to run.
You'll make many friends. **You'll have lots of fun."**

Mike grabbed a pillow and covered his head.
"I'm too scared to try it. I'm staying in bed."

Then right in Mike's room, a fierce battle grew.
Fire-breathing dragons marched in two by two.

The dragons made noise, and Mike covered his ears.
He squeezed his eyes shut and trembled with fear.

From off in the distance the Dragon King said,
"Hey, Mike, get your booty up out of that bed.

Adventures await you. It's your turn to fly.
Now throw off those blankets and give it a try."

Mike furrowed his forehead. "Oh, what should I do?
Can I fly like the dragons? What if that's true?"

Mike leaped out of bed. "I do want to fly.
It sounds so exciting. I'll give it a try."

The Dragon King roared, "Today is the day of the big dragon race.
Hop up on my back, and we'll try for first place."

Mike thought the dragons were all set to go,
But a small one looked frightened and shook his head no.

"Little dragon," Mike said in a voice loud and clear.
"Just smile and say 'hi,' and there's nothing to fear."

The little guy turned and smiled up at Mike.
"Hey, kid," the King nodded. "Now that's what I like."

DRAGON
RACE

Mike scrambled up. The Dragon King roared.
Loud whistles blew, and away they all soared.

Out of Mike's room and all over the town,
Mike giggled with glee as he bounced up and down.

The King breathed fire. Mike yelled, "There's my school!
See the swings and the sandbox? Wow, this is so cool."

The dragons dipped down like a colorful cloud.
They zoomed past the school, and Mike chuckled out loud.

Then the King flew so fast no one else could keep pace.
"We did it!" Mike shouted. "We just won the race!"

The next day on the playground, Mike saw a new girl.
He heard the King whisper, "Kid, give it a whirl."

Mike smiled a big smile and made himself say,
"Hi, I'm Mike. Do you want to play?"

"I'm Chloe," she said. "Let's try something new.
I can hang by my knees. It's not hard to do.

One leg at a time while you hold the bar tight,
Then drop both your hands—oh, you got it just right!"

I did it, Mike thought, gazing up at the sky.
I hung by my knees, and I smiled and said, "hi."

The
End

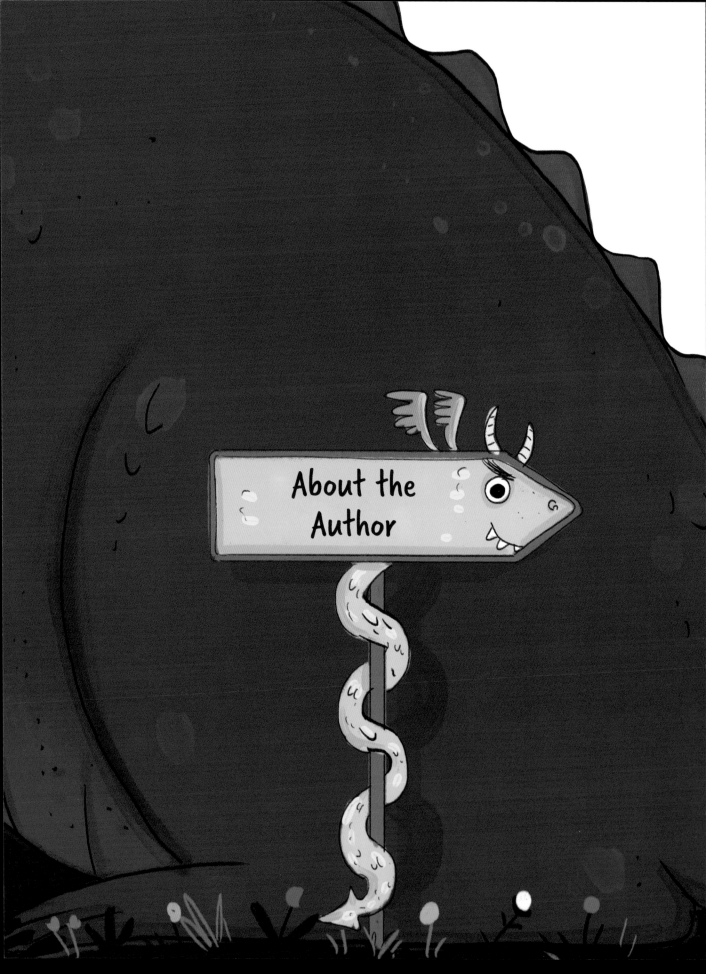

Mary Jo Hazard, MA, MFT, is a retired marriage and family therapist with thirty years of experience working with children. She was a consultant for Brighter Days Montessori School, a therapist at Cedar House (a child abuse treatment center), and a child therapist at Charter Hospital. In 2010, Mary Jo published her first children's book, *The Peacocks of Palos Verdes*. She followed the peacock book with *Palo's World*, a picture book about a little peacock growing up in the Palos Verdes area, and *P is for Palos Verdes*, a photo essay of the peninsula's most famous attractions. *Stillwater*, her coming-of-age novel, was released on Amazon as a #1 best seller in July 2020. She is a popular presenter in local preschool and elementary schools and a regular contributor to *Peninsula News*. She loves living on the Palos Verdes Peninsula—a place with crashing waves, rolling hills, and colorful peacocks in the trees.